MAX AN...

SPACE

ADVENTURE

BY SAMANTHA METCALF

ILLUSTRATED BY IAN R. WARD

First published in Great Britain in 2017 by:
Mysteries in Time Limited
info@mysteriesintime.com

Reprinted 2021

Illustrated by Ian R. Ward
www.ianrward.co.uk

A catalogue record for this book is available from the British Library.

ISBN 978-1-9997257-0-9

Hi! I'm Katie and I am 8 years old. I think my favourite thing is playing outside in any weather. I love going to the park, especially the adventure playground with the huge, curly slide. You can go really fast on that one, especially when you lie down!

Mum hates it when I come home covered in mud, but I can't help it. The fun parts of the park are always the muddiest.

Max is my older brother. He's really clever. He helps me with my homework when I'm stuck. He knows everything! But don't tell him I said that.

My brother always looks out for me. And we have lots of fun playing games together.

Hey, I'm Max and I'm 11. I love reading. I read comics and cartoons that make me laugh, and I read adventure stories about knights and castles, or pirates and buried treasure.

I also love solving puzzles. Grandpa always buys me books full of word-searches and crosswords. I like to time myself and see how fast I can solve them.

Katie is my younger sister. She is really energetic and fun to be around, even though she can't sit still for more than five minutes! She's really fast and sporty. I wish I could be as good as her at sports. But don't tell her I said that.

1

"Look out!" yelled Max.

It felt like time stood still as he watched Katie fall backwards.

They were in the back garden with Grandpa, admiring the night sky. Grandpa had set his telescope up on its tripod at the end of the garden, hoping to see Mars. According to the lady on the News, there was an excellent chance of seeing the Red Planet tonight.

Grandpa had spent the last thirty minutes teaching Max how to read the stars.

"The stars are like a map," he had explained. "You can see patterns between different stars. These patterns or groups of stars are called constellations." Grandpa pointed to three stars in a row, as if drawn in a straight line. "That's called Orion's Belt. The full constellation is called Orion, named after a hunter in Ancient Greek mythology. Those three stars make up his belt."

Max saw the three stars with his naked eye, then peered through the telescope to look more closely. As he did, something caught his eye.

"Look!" he exclaimed. "It's a shooting star!"

Grandpa smiled. "Actually, that's the

International Space Station as it orbits the Earth. It travels all the way round the globe nearly sixteen times a day."

Max scratched his head. "Don't they get dizzy?"

Grandpa laughed. "No, I don't think they feel like they are moving that fast. They probably feel like they are standing still and it's the Earth that is whizzing past them!"

Meanwhile, Katie was bored waiting for her turn to look through the telescope. She had brought some peanuts with her and was throwing them in the air and catching them in her mouth one by one. She was getting better and better at it, even in the dim light of the moon.

She started to get bolder, started to throw them higher and higher. She now threw one so high, that she lost it for a moment amongst the stars in the sky above her. When she spotted it again, she imagined it was a star falling down to Earth. She had thrown it too far; she had to take a step back, then another.

She hadn't checked behind her, hadn't realised how close she was to Max and the telescope, not until it was too late.

Max called out as Katie's left leg hit the tripod and she lost her balance. She stumbled backwards, landing on the soft grass with a thump. Grandpa had pulled the telescope to safety just in time.

Katie threw her hands in the air triumphantly.

"What are you cheering about?" asked Max.

"I caught the falling star, even though I was falling at the same time!" she exclaimed.

Max rolled his eyes. Sometimes he just didn't understand his sister.

It was like she was from another planet.

2

Clouds had moved across the sky, putting an end to their hopes of seeing Mars tonight. But Max had seen so many other things tonight that he really didn't mind.

"Thanks Grandpa!" he said as they packed up the telescope. "Can we do this again tomorrow night?"

Grandpa smiled. "Of course, Max."

Katie skipped ahead as they all went back inside, where Mum was waiting with cups of hot chocolate.

"I have a surprise for you," she said happily. "I was shopping when the postman came today, but our neighbour has just brought round a parcel for you."

Mum produced a turquoise box and Max and Katie squealed with delight. Max picked up the box and bounced upstairs. Katie carried their hot chocolates behind him, concentrating carefully.

They quickly found the Mission Plan.

Mission Plan

Place: Mir Space Station
Date: AD 1991

The Mir Space Station had recently welcomed
astronauts from outside the USSR. For the
first time in decades, Russians were working
alongside Americans and Europeans. For most
people, this was a positive step towards
a peaceful future. However, many people in
America and Europe still didn't trust the
Russians, and many in Russia refused to trust
the West.

In 1991, things keep breaking on board the
Mir Space Station and Michael, the American
engineer, gets the blame. He is sure he keeps
fixing things. However, when they break again
he starts to doubt himself. Is Michael losing
his mind, or is he being framed?

Task:

Can you find out whether Michael is simply
forgetful or whether someone else is making
him look bad at his job? If so, what is the
reason? Find out before everyone's lives
are put in serious danger and before the
engineer is sent back to Earth as a disgraced
astronaut.

3

Max and Katie's eyes were like saucers. They were speechless, even Katie!

They were going to the Mir Space Station.

They were going into space.

They were going to be astronauts!

Max was jumping up and down in excitement, while Katie did her Excited Dance. Normally, this dance caused Max to double over with laughter, but he was so busy imagining what it would be like to float without gravity that he didn't even notice.

They were brought back to reality when they heard Mum's concerned voice calling from downstairs. "Are you two OK?"

Max stopped jumping and held up his hand to signal to Katie to stop dancing.

"Yes Mum," he called back. "We were just dancing!"

They heard Mum laugh, then listened carefully as she returned to her conversation with Grandpa in the kitchen.

Max and Katie took deep breaths to calm down and sat down on the carpet. They knew they had to learn as much as they could before they travelled to the Space Station, but it was difficult to concentrate.

Max opened up the history booklet and read all about space. They learnt about how the navigators in the 16th century used the stars to find their way around the globe. They learnt about the Cold War and how it created a Space Race. They read about Yuri Gagarin and Neil Armstrong and about the planets. Finally, they read about gravity and how it felt to float in space.

"Do you think we'll meet some aliens?" asked Katie.

Max laughed. "No, I don't think any aliens have been discovered."

"Not that we know of," she corrected.

Max looked inside the box again and found the Time Travel Sticker. It was a Space Shuttle.

"Very cool," he said as he passed it to Katie.

Katie nodded her head in agreement.

"What should we wear?" asked Katie anxiously. "I don't think we'll be able to find proper space suits anywhere, not ones that will help us in space."

That was a good question. Max looked again at the Mission Plan. He turned it over and was surprised to see an extra note.

The Time Machine will transport you to the airlock between the Space Shuttle and the Mir Space Station. Your space suits will be inside the airlock.

The real visiting astronauts have fallen sick and cannot travel onto the Space Station for three hours. You will take their place by pretending to be the new astronauts. You will have only three hours to solve this mystery, before the real astronauts feel better and visit the Space Station. You must solve the mystery and disappear before this happens.

Good Luck.

Max and Katie were silent for a few minutes as they both thought about how difficult this mission could be.

Max had a gulp of his hot chocolate, which wasn't very hot any more. "Well, at least we don't need to find a space suit," he said. "Clothes in the 1990s weren't very different to our clothes. We can just wear t-shirts, jeans and trainers."

Katie looked Max up and down, then checked what she was wearing in the mirror. She nodded. "Then we're ready to go!"

Max programmed the Time Machine to take them to the Mir Space Station in 1991 and Katie pushed the large red button on top.

"Here goes!" grinned Max.

4

Max and Katie felt the ground swirl away from beneath their feet as the Time Machine took them on the journey through history.

This time, it felt different. There was no pulling sensation as gravity took control of them; there was no solid ground forming beneath their feet. Instead, it felt as though they were lost in Time and a moment of panic and fear crept over Max.

Suddenly, solid walls started to form around them and they realised they weren't lost in Time, they were floating in zero-gravity!

Max looked around. They were in a small space with round doors at each end. There were warning lights that told them the doors must stay locked while the pressure between the two capsules was made equal. There were long, important-looking cables that ran along the wall in clumps as large as tree trunks. Max realised he was still holding his breath and let out a burst of air.

He grinned at Katie. "We're in space!"

Katie was looking green. Max understood immediately.

"It can take time to get used to the feeling of weightlessness," he explained gently. "It's normal to feel a bit sick at first, but you'll get used to it."

He tried to distract her with the space suits that were floating next to them. "Look, Katie!" he exclaimed. "These are our space suits!"

Max peered at the suits and realised they were like overalls or jumpsuits. He unzipped the front and stepped his legs inside, which sent him spinning round slowly like he was doing a somersault. Max hated spinning. He couldn't stand those fairground rides that spin you round and round, since they make him feel sick. He had once thrown up all over the feet of the fairground attendant as he climbed off the ride. That feeling was back now.

Katie saw Max's expression change and knew he was starting to feel sick. She did wonder for a moment what would happen if he were sick in space. Where would the sick go? Would it float around in a giant blob until it bumped into the space shuttle walls - or themselves? Would it separate into tiny sick-coloured droplets and spread out?

She shuddered and realised she was already feeling better herself and that she had to help Max. She reached out to the wall to steady herself, then with the other hand reached out to Max and gently stopped him from spinning.

Max smiled gratefully and finished pulling his suit over his clothes, while Katie held him steady. They then swapped round, with Max keeping Katie steady as she got dressed.

They looked the part now!

"How come we don't have the full suit with the

helmet?" asked Katie.

"That's what the astronauts wear when they do a spacewalk," explained Max.

Katie moved her legs as if she were walking in mid-air. "Like this?"

Max laughed. "No! A spacewalk is when they step outside the Space Station to fix something. They need to wear those helmets so they can breathe. We have oxygen pumped inside the shuttle and the Space Station, so we don't need it," replied Max. "Besides, we would be really clumsy with one of those suits on in here!"

Just then, they heard a bang and a strange creaking noise. Max and Katie looked at each other anxiously.

That didn't sound good.

5

Max and Katie looked towards the source of the noise. It was coming from one of the round doors. They saw a light turn from red to green, then watched the large handle start to turn as if by magic.

"It's the aliens!" shrieked Katie. "I knew it! They can move metal with their minds!"

Max smiled. "It's not aliens. It's being opened from the other side. We're about to meet the astronauts on board the Mir Space Station!"

Katie watched as the door opened and a smiling face peered in at them.

"Welcome to Mir," she said with a Russian accent. "Come through and meet the team!"

Max and Katie pushed the wall to propel themselves in the right direction. Katie pushed a little too hard at first and bumped her shoulder on the edge of the hatch.

"Don't worry, you'll get used to moving about in here," smiled the kind lady.

Once they were through, they watched the same lady close the hatch door. She then pushed a few buttons and typed a code into a computer.

"My name is Nina and I am in charge of all communications with Earth," she explained.

Nina then introduced them to the three other crew members of the Mir Space Station.

She pointed to a large man with a heavy-looking camcorder. "This is Ivan, my fellow Russian cosmonaut."

Ivan waved at them, but didn't remove the camcorder from his shoulder. The small red light was flashing, which meant he was filming. Katie flicked her hair and smiled at the camera like a film star.

Nina moved on to another man. "This is our American friend, Michael."

Michael waved. "Hi there! Welcome to Mir."

Max and Katie both knew that Michael was the engineer they were here to investigate. They smiled and waved back.

"And finally, here's Pierre from France. Pierre is our space biologist."

Pierre waved at Max and Katie, who smiled back.

Suddenly, their introductions were interrupted by a piercing sound all around them.

It was an alarm.

Something was very wrong.

6

The crew got straight to work. Max and Katie watched as they launched themselves expertly in different directions and set to work at computers, pushing buttons and switches while speaking to Ground Control through headsets with microphones.

Max and Katie felt helpless as they watched and waited.

They suddenly felt very far from home.

Thankfully, it wasn't long before the alarm and the red light stopped and the crew all breathed a sigh of relief.

"Panic over!" said Pierre. "It was just a small problem."

Max laughed. "All that noise for just a small problem?!"

Pierre smiled. "It does sound a bit worrying when

you first hear the alarm, but you'll get used to it,"
he said. "It's just a loose screw on the control panel.
Nothing dangerous."

Katie noticed that Michael's reaction was
different to everyone else's.

He was scratching his head and frowning.

"But I fixed that yesterday," he said to the
crew. "You must remember? After the first alarm, I
tightened that same screw. Honestly I did!"

Katie saw that everyone nodded and smiled politely at Michael, but quickly moved away to get on with their own work.

Max and Katie watched Michael's shoulders slump as he picked up a screwdriver and tightened the loose screw.

"All fixed," he said quietly. "Again."

Max wanted to find out more. "Have many things been going wrong on board the Space Station recently?"

Michael nodded. "Small things. It's never anything that will put the crew's lives in danger, just things that make day-to-day tasks more difficult. For example, some wires were disconnected in the biology experiment that Pierre is working on. Some lights in the sleep stations stopped working. Small screws become loose, like this one."

"Could it become loose by itself?" asked Katie.

Michael shook his head. "No, these parts are

designed to withstand all sorts of intense pressure and movement. They can only be loosened by hand."

"Why would anyone want to cause these small problems?" asked Max.

"I have no idea!" exclaimed Michael, throwing his hands in the air. "We all work hard. We all know how lucky we are to be here. It's a once-in-a-lifetime trip. Why would anyone want to sabotage that?"

Max knew Michael was right.

It didn't make any sense.

7

Michael explained that he had to get on with his daily exercise routine and floated away to a different section.

"Exercise?!" exclaimed Katie. "How can you exercise in space?"

"They have treadmills that they strap you to," explained Max. "Astronauts have to exercise for two hours every day."

"Two hours?! Wow!" replied Katie. "They must be really fit and strong when they get back to Earth."

Max smiled. "They don't exercise to become athletes, they exercise to stop their muscles wasting away. When you can float everywhere, you're not using your legs. You're not even standing! So they have to work every day to build up the muscle."

Katie didn't think it sounded like much fun having to walk for two hours every day but never get anywhere.

They realised they were alone. Max smiled at Katie and pushed himself gently into the middle of the capsule. He bent his knees and dipped his head forward, which made him do a slow-motion somersault.

Katie laughed and decided to try something she had always wanted to try: fly like Superman. She pulled herself along the walls until she was at the furthest end of the capsule, held one arm ahead of her with her fist clenched, then launched herself forward. She flew the whole length without bumping into anything, while Max sang the Superman theme tune badly.

"I love being in space!" laughed Katie as she came to a gentle stop near Max.

Pierre floated past at this point and smiled when he saw Max and Katie practising in weightlessness.

"Have you tried drinking water yet?" he asked.

Max and Katie shook their heads.

"No, but I am quite thirsty after our acrobatics!"
said Max.

Pierre gave them each a pouch with a cap.

"Watch me first, then try," he said.

He squeezed the pouch gently until a drop of
water flew out and floated in mid-air. Pierre smiled
at them as he lifted his head and caught the drop in
his mouth.

"It's just like catching peanuts!" laughed Katie.

Max and Katie both had a go and were delighted when they caught the drop of water in their mouths.

Pierre waved at them as he continued his journey along the capsule.

Max and Katie started playing a game. Max squeezed a drop of water and - just before it came loose - he pushed the pouch in Katie's direction. This launched the drop of water towards Katie and they both watched it tumble through the capsule, never breaking apart. Katie was ready: she caught it in her mouth and Max cheered!

It was Max's turn. Katie followed Max's example and launched a drop of water in Max's direction. Max pushed himself in the right direction, but missed. The drop landed on Max's nose instead and clung there on his skin! They were both laughing, when the alarm sounded again.

What could be wrong this time?

8

Max and Katie watched as everyone rushed past them, checking different switches, buttons and computers. They didn't have to wait long before the alarm went quiet. Everyone looked around to see who had found the problem.

Michael reappeared, his face pale.

"I know what the problem is," he said nervously. "It's the same screw that was loose earlier. It had somehow become loose again. I've fixed it now. Again."

This time, nobody tried to be polite. They shook their heads and turned their backs on Michael as they returned to their work.

Michael looked defeated.

"I did tighten it before, he said quietly to himself. "I know I did."

He must have forgotten that Max and Katie were

there, because he jumped when Max spoke.

"We believe you," said Max. "We saw you fix it with a screwdriver after the first alarm."

Michael's face lit up with hope. "Yes! You were there! That means I'm not going mad!"

Katie thought for a moment. "But that means someone else keeps sabotaging equipment on purpose," she said. "Why would they want to frame you?"

Michael shrugged again. "I have no idea. But I know nobody trusts me any more. I will be sent back to Earth soon if things continue to go wrong."

"Don't worry, we will help investigate," assured Max. "We will find out who is framing you and why."

Max looked around, trying to think where to start. His eyes landed on a familiar-looking object in the corner.

"What about the cameras that are inside the

space station?" asked Max. "Are they always filming?"

Michael's eyes widened. "Yes!" he replied. "They should be working."

Michael pulled himself towards the nearest computer and started typing codes and instructions.

"Can you see the camera footage from the moments when the alarms sounded?" asked Katie.

"I hope so," he replied, but his hopes were quickly dashed when he opened the camera logs.

Michael was frowning. "No. Someone has deleted the footage from those times. Someone is covering their tracks."

"Who has access to the camera logs?" asked Max, hoping this would narrow it down.

"Everyone," replied Michael.

9

Max and Katie agreed to split up to investigate. They only had a few hours left before the real crew from the Space Shuttle would recover and appear.

Katie found Nina, the friendly Russian cosmonaut who had introduced everyone. She was tapping busily on a computer.

"Ah, hello Katie," she said brightly. "How are you settling in? Are you getting used to zero-gravity yet?"

Katie smiled. "It takes a bit of getting used to, but it is fun once you know how to move!"

"It's wonderful to have some British people on board. It was a distant dream a few years ago to be working together with so many other countries. The Cold War was a terrible time. Nobody trusted each other. I'm so happy those years are over. We can look forward to a brighter future where all countries can work together for the good of mankind."

Katie smiled and nodded her head. She looked over Nina's shoulder. "What are you working on?"

Katie was hoping to see that Nina was looking at the camera files so she could solve the mystery straight away and enjoy the rest of the time in space. Instead, Nina was working on complicated graphs.

"This is a record of our communication systems with Ground Control back on Earth. We need to monitor how well our computers communicate with the computers back on Earth. If there are any problems, we may need to do a spacewalk to repair anything that's broken."

Katie was imagining floating outside the Space Station, when her eyes were drawn to something that was catching the light. Nina had screwdrivers and spanners in her pocket.

"Er, Nina, do you ever have to do repairs yourself, inside the Space Station?" she asked.

Nina didn't take her eyes off the screen. "Oh yes! My computer keyboard often breaks. All it needs is a little tightening up, nothing too complicated. That's why I carry these tools around with me all the time."

Nina patted the pocket with her right hand then continued typing.

Katie decided to ask her about Michael. "What do you think is going wrong with all these alarms?"

"Oh, I'm sure they are just simple mistakes," she replied. "We're all human, we all make mistakes! Besides, this Space Station is strong, but things will naturally start to break. It's just a shame that at the moment it's only things that Michael has worked on. It will be something I do wrong tomorrow. Or Pierre. Or Ivan. I hope Michael doesn't feel too bad about it."

Katie believed Nina. She seemed genuinely concerned about Michael.

"I look forward to spending some time with

you later, Katie," said Nina cheerfully. "We should celebrate this joyful occasion of becoming a fully international crew on board Mir!"

Katie left Nina to work in peace. She had tools that could be used to carry out the sabotage, but Katie had no idea what motive she might have.

10

Max went in search of the other Russian crew member, Ivan. He was resting and listening to music in a quiet section of the Space Station.

"Er, hi Ivan, sorry to disturb you," said Max.

Ivan opened one eye, looked at Max then closed it again without replying.

Max didn't know what to do. He wanted to leave, but he knew they were running out of time to help Michael.

"Er, what do you think about the alarms sounding all the time?" he asked nervously.

Ivan took a deep breath then replied, like it was a huge effort to speak. "That American is a fool," he replied. "He should not be here. I know hundreds of Russian cosmonauts who should be here instead of him. This is a Russian Space Station. It should be full of Russian cosmonauts."

Max suddenly felt very unwelcome.

He thought about what Ivan had said. He definitely had motive: he thought only Russian cosmonauts should be allowed on this Space Station. Perhaps he was sabotaging Michael's work so he could convince Ground Control that bringing different countries together was a mistake?

Max suddenly remembered that Ivan usually had a camcorder on his shoulder. He would definitely know how to delete camera footage.

11

Katie had left Nina and was now talking to Pierre, the French biologist. Pierre was concentrating on one of his experiments.

"Ah, bonjour Katie!" smiled Pierre. "Would you like to see what I am investigating?"

Katie could see some new plants growing. She had grown some pretty flowers at school last year in the summer term. They had been learning all about the life cycle of a plant, how it grows, what it needs to grow. She remembered being amazed at how quickly it grew from a simple seed into a shoot, then how it bloomed into a flower.

"Yes please," she said enthusiastically.

"I am investigating the effect of growing plants in space. We want to find out whether plants we grow here are as safe to eat as plants grown under natural conditions on Earth," explained Pierre.

"Why do you want to find that out?" asked Katie.

"In the future, it's possible that there will be missions deeper into space, longer missions," replied Pierre. "It would be even more important for astronauts to grow as much of their own food as possible. I am also trying to find out if a particular kind of heat lamp works better than another."

Katie admired the tanks full of plants. It was like a mini greenhouse.

"Just one more thing," she continued. "What do you think is happening with all these alarms?"

Pierre sighed. "It's very sad. I believe Michael is an excellent engineer. But space has affected him and made him forgetful. It's the only explanation. He's a kind man and I know he would never do this on purpose. We all need to support him and help him get used to being on the Space Station. I am sure he will be better with time. It is important we make this mission a success."

12

Max and Katie found each other in a quiet part of the Space Station and shared what they had learnt.

"Nina seems very excited about being on board Mir with different nationalities," started Katie. "She seemed sympathetic and understanding about Michael. She thinks it's just human nature to make mistakes. And she's right!"

"But we know Michael didn't make a mistake," reminded Max. "We saw him fix that loose screw."

"Oh yes, true. It's just easy to think it's a big misunderstanding!" replied Katie. "The only thing suspicious is the fact that she carries a spanner and a screwdriver in her pocket all the time. She could have sabotaged the equipment."

Max was nodding.

"Well Ivan was very different to Nina," continued

Max. "He was very unwelcoming. He thinks there should only be Russians on board Mir. He has real motive to frame an American astronaut and make him look bad. Plus he is a cameraman, so he would definitely know how to delete camera footage."

Katie agreed. Ivan seemed suspicious.

"Then there is Pierre," she said. "He also seems sympathetic about Michael. He thinks space has affected his memory, but that he will get better with time. He is busy carrying out biology investigations. I can't think of any reason why he would want to frame Michael."

Max sighed. "If only we had that camera footage!"

Katie had an idea. "What about Ivan's camcorder footage? He was filming everything earlier when we arrived and he still had the camcorder when the alarm sounded. Perhaps he caught something suspicious on there?"

Max grinned. "That's a great idea Sis'!" he said. "If he says 'no', then we can guess he has something to hide."

"And if that part of the footage has been deleted, then that also points to his guilt!"

They both pushed themselves off the nearest wall in the direction of where Ivan was relaxing.

"Hi Ivan," said Max cheerfully. He felt much more confident now that Katie was with him and they had a plan.

Ivan opened his eyes slowly and glared at Max.

"We need your help," explained Katie. "We know that Michael is being framed. We were with him when he tightened that screw earlier, but somehow it became loose again. Someone else on this Space Station is making Michael look bad. We think your camcorder footage can help find the guilty person."

Max expected Ivan to look angry. Instead, he raised his eyebrows. He looked interested.

"You think I may have accidentally filmed someone breaking the equipment on purpose?" he asked.

Max nodded. "Will you help us?"

Ivan didn't say anything, but he reached for his camcorder and turned it on. He pressed rewind and Katie heard a strange whizzing noise.

"What's that noise?" she asked.

Max smiled. "It's the cassette tape inside the camcorder."

Katie had only ever seen digital cameras before. She had heard stories from Mum and Grandpa about the olden days, when cameras used film that could be ruined if exposed to sunlight, and films and music were recorded on cassette tapes, but she had never seen one.

Ivan finished rewinding and pressed play. Katie squealed with delight when she saw herself and Max first appear through the airlock door.

"We're not here to admire ourselves, Katie. We're here to find the person who is framing Michael," reminded Max.

Ivan actually smiled when he heard this, but continued watching the camera carefully.

They kept watching, all the way until the alarm sounded. Nothing.

All their feelings of hope were dashed. They had no idea how they would ever find out who was guilty.

Just then, Ivan rewound the footage.

"Did you see something?" asked Max.

Ivan pressed play. "Look."

They watched carefully, but the only thing they could see was themselves doing somersaults and catching water in their mouths.

"That's just us," replied Katie putting her hands on her hips. "I hope you don't think we are guilty."

Ivan rewound it again. "Look carefully," he said.

"Look at the window."

Max and Katie leaned closer to the screen. They realised what Ivan was pointing at. There was the reflection of someone near the screw that kept getting loosened. The reflection was clear enough to see the person's face as they turned to check they weren't being watched.

They knew who was framing Michael.

13

Max and Katie thanked Ivan for his help, then they all went to find the rest of the crew. They gathered together near the scene of the crime: the mysteriously loose screw.

Everyone looked confused about why they were gathered together.

"We only arrived today, but it was clear there was something wrong on this Space Station," started Max. "Mir is only a few years old; things shouldn't be breaking so often, especially not when they have just been fixed!"

Michael lowered his eyes in embarrassment.

"Michael has been getting the blame for everything going wrong," continued Katie. "But Michael is innocent. He has been working hard to fix the things that have gone wrong, only for them to go wrong again."

"Somebody here has been sabotaging the equipment and pointing the blame at Michael," agreed Katie.

Everyone looked around at each other suspiciously.

"We know who did it, we just don't understand why," said Max. "Perhaps you can explain why you did it, Pierre?"

Nina's hand flew to her mouth as she gasped in shock. Michael's eyes widened as he heard Pierre's name called out.

Pierre's eyes narrowed. "I don't know what you're talking about," he said.

Ivan shook his head. "We have proof, Pierre. You cannot deny it. We have video footage on the camcorder."

"Why, Pierre?" asked Michael. "What did I ever do to you?"

Pierre folded his arms. "It was never about you,

Michael. I'm sorry that you were being blamed. That was never my plan. It just happened that the easiest things to tamper with fell under your control."

"But why tamper with anything?" asked Nina.

"My experiments are my life's work," explained Pierre. "I am expected to have results when I get home. The company that makes one of the heat lamps will pay me lots of money if my experiments prove that their heat lamp is the best. I already promised them that it would be. I really thought it would be! But my predictions were wrong. I have made a terrible mistake."

"But that's OK," said Katie. "What does it matter that your predictions were wrong? It happens all the time in science."

Pierre shook his head. "You don't understand. I have already accepted money from this company. A lot of money. They are expecting the results and I need to give them the right answer."

Pierre was starting to sweat. Max could see that he was really worried about what would happen when he returned, but he still didn't understand.

"But why tamper with equipment? What good would that do?" asked Max.

"I had to change the results of the experiments. The only way to do this was to turn off the other lamp from time to time," explained Pierre. "But somebody would notice if I kept doing this. I had to disguise it as an accident by turning off other things too. I had to pretend there were lots of things breaking, not just my lamps."

Katie felt bad for Pierre. He wasn't a bad person. He had made a mistake but got caught in a mess of lies, trying to cover up his mistake.

"What will happen now?" asked Katie.

Ivan took a deep breath. "I'm sorry, Pierre, but you will be sent back to Earth. You will have to tell the truth to everyone there. I don't think anyone needs to know about the broken equipment or the sabotage. That can stay our little secret, if everyone agrees?"

Ivan looked around at everyone, who nodded their agreement.

"However, you will have to be honest with that company and tell them the truth. Perhaps they can change the design of their lamp to make it better. You may have done them a favour," finished Ivan.

Pierre looked relieved and surprised.

"Thank you Ivan," he said. "Thank you everyone. That is very kind of you, especially you Michael. You didn't have to agree to this, especially after what I put you through. I wish things had been different."

Max and Katie watched as everyone said goodbye to Pierre, then turned to Michael to apologise.

"I'm sorry I ever doubted you, Michael," said Nina.

Michael smiled and thanked her, then turned to Max and Katie.

"Thank you for helping me," he said. "I am so grateful to you. I don't know how I can ever repay you."

"We're just happy the mystery was solved and you can get on with enjoying your time in space," replied Max.

14

Max and Katie knew their time on board the Mir Space Station was nearly over and they wanted to do one last thing.

They pulled themselves over to the nearest window and saw the Earth whiz past. It was the most beautiful thing they had ever seen. Grandpa

was right: it felt like they were standing still and the Earth was rushing past.

"Look!" exclaimed Max. "That's Europe!"

"It looks just like the map on our wall at home!" replied Katie. "The sea looks so blue and the land looks so green. It's funny that we can't see any people, even as tiny dots."

"We're just too far away," said Max. "Looking down at the Earth like this makes me realise how small we are in the universe."

Katie nodded. It was a strange feeling, knowing that a younger Mum and a younger Grandpa were down there right now somewhere. Normally when they travelled through time they went so far back that nobody they knew had been born yet.

Their thoughts were interrupted by surprised voices.

They looked round and realised what had happened. The airlock was finally pressurised enough to open the hatch door. Pierre had collected his belongings and said his goodbyes, before getting ready to enter the Shuttle to return to Earth. As the hatch door was opened, everyone was shocked to see two faces there, smiling and moving onto the Space Station.

"Who are you?" exclaimed Ivan. "There were only supposed to be two new astronauts arriving on this Shuttle. Where did you come from?"

The two new faces looked confused. "Yes, there were only supposed to be two of us," laughed one of them "And there are only two of us!"

Ivan shook his head. "No. There are four of you. We have already met Max and Katie, now you are two more."

The new astronauts shook their heads. "Who are Max and Katie? We don't know Max or Katie."

The Space Station fell silent. You could have heard a pin drop. Everyone turned to face Max and

Katie, who were stunned into silence. They didn't know what to say. They had been discovered.

Just then, there were flashes of light in front of their eyes. It felt like the stars had somehow travelled through the walls of the Space Station and were forming around them. Max and Katie knew they were being wrapped in the swirl of Time Travel and took one last look around. Everyone looked shocked, amazed, scared.

Within moments, they had returned to Max's

bedroom. It was strange to feel the floor beneath their feet. It reminded Katie of swimming in the sea then returning to the beach; you still feel like you are bobbing in the waves even after you are back on dry land.

Max suddenly started giggling. "Did you see their faces?"

"They looked terrified," replied Katie. "Do you think they will think we were aliens?"

Max nodded. "There may be a Top Secret file somewhere that suggests aliens exist, aliens that look like humans but can teleport and disappear into thin air!"

"Or they will agree to keep it secret," suggested Katie. "Like they agreed to keep Pierre's actions secret."

Max shrugged. "I guess we'll never know!"

Also in the Mysteries in Time series:

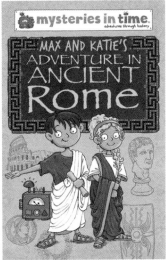